To Dad - for all the wheelbarrow rides.

A TEMPLAR BOOK
First published in the UK in 2005 by Templar Publishing,
an imprint of The Templar Company plc,
Pippbrook Mill, London Road, Dorking, Surrey, RH4 1JE, UK
www.templarco.co.uk

1 3 5 7 9 10 8 6 4 2

ISBN 1-84011-342-1

Designed by Andy Mansfield
Edited by Sue Harris

Printed in China

a goodnight warren book

Warren and the
Great Carrot Race

Liane Payne

templar publishing

Warren the Rabbit loved his vegetable patch. Every year he grew lots of tasty things: cabbages in the spring; lettuce in the summer; sprouts in the autumn and, of course, carrots! Carrots were Warren's favourite food and he always grew a handsome crop.

Warren's Uncle Albert was a prize-winning gardener, too. He lived next door and was full of useful gardening tips.

"Plant marigolds round your cabbages to keep the slugs away!" he'd say. "And don't forget to dig some compost in before you plant your carrots. Then they'll grow big and juicy!"

Warren's Auntie May was full of useful advice, too. "Never leave carrots in the ground after the first frost. Bring them to me and I'll make them into a carrot cake for you."

Warren licked his lips. Aunt May's cakes were so tasty!

One Autumn morning weeks later Warren woke early. Outside, the sun was shining, but one sniff of the air told him that the first frosts of winter were on their way. "It's time to harvest my carrot crop," said Warren, collecting his trusty old wheelbarrow and fork from the shed. He was just about to start digging when his friend Pippy the Squirrel arrived.

"Oh Warren, can you help me?" asked Pippy anxiously. "I need to put my nut store somewhere safe before winter. If I could use your wheelbarrow, it would be done in no time!"

"Of course, Pippy," Warren said kindly, and by teatime the nuts were all safely stored in a hole in the old oak tree.

The next day Warren was up bright and early, determined to catch up on his digging. But it wasn't long before Gus the Mole came calling.

"I'm making a new tunnel for winter, but I'm so cold that I can't dig properly," complained Gus. "Do you think you could help me?"

Now Warren really wanted to get on with his own digging, but poor Gus looked so miserable he couldn't refuse.

"Of course I'll help," he said, handing Gus his scarf to warm him up.

It took Warren all day to dig Gus's tunnel and the next day it was colder than ever. 'I must get those carrots up before the ground completely freezes,' thought Warren. But then – disaster struck! The wheel of the barrow hit a stone and, with an almighty crack, off it came. "Now what shall I do?" cried Warren miserably.

Luckily, help was at hand. "You've helped us!" said Pippy and Gus. "Now, it's our turn to help you!" Uncle Albert took charge and soon everyone was digging up carrots. "We'd best get them into the shed as quick as we can. I think it's going to snow!" he said.

"I know, let's see who can move the biggest pile of carrots," suggested Uncle Albert. "The winner gets a special prize!" And so the Great Carrot Race began... The friends ran up and down Warren's garden, carrying as many carrots as they could.

In no time all the carrots were safely stored in Warren's shed. And guess who had moved the biggest pile? Why, Warren, of course! "And here's your prize!" laughed Auntie May. She had baked the BIGGEST carrot cake Warren had ever seen! Soon, they were all inside by the fire, munching carrot cake and sipping mugs of hot tea.

Since then, whenever his carrot crop is ready, Warren always invites his friends round for a Carrot Race, even though Uncle Albert made him a brand new wheelbarrow. Warren always wins and Auntie May always bakes a carrot cake as his prize.

"It's much more fun than digging up carrots on your own..." says Warren.

"But just as tiring," he adds, as he snuggles
down for a well-earned sleep.
Goodnight, Warren!

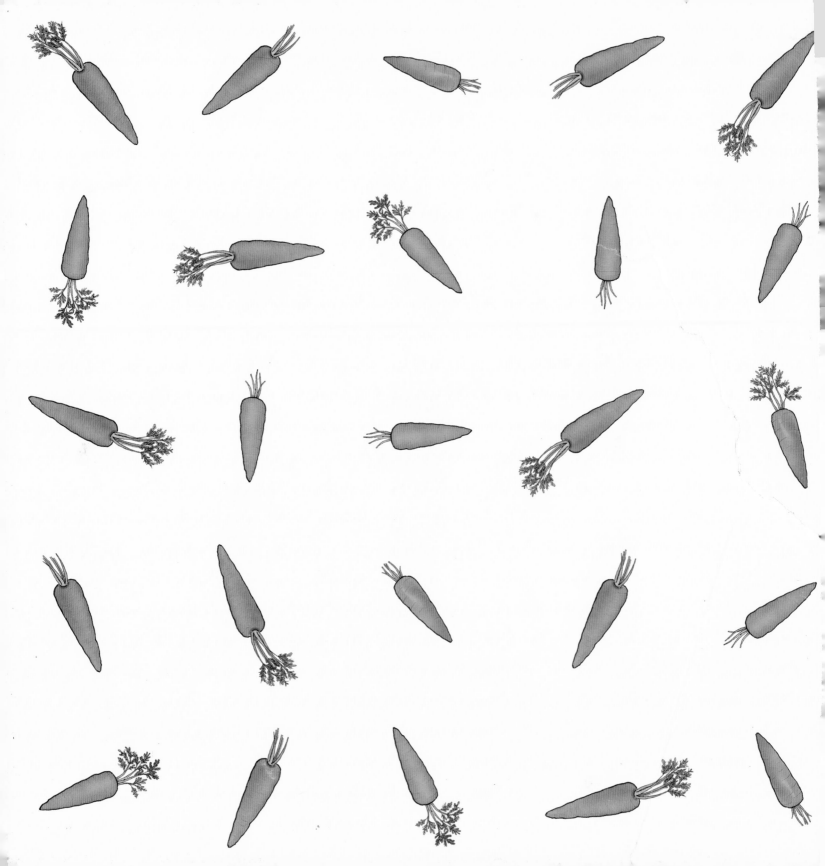